Sebastian

The Cat That Never Shaved

Faye Thompson
2015

CHILDREN'S NOW YOU KNOW SERIES
BOOK ONE

Sebastian
The Cat That Never Shaved

by Faye Thompson

Illustrations by Bryan Thackeray

Once upon a time there was a big black and white cat named Sebastian. Sebastian was different from most cats because his whiskers grew very long and sometimes he would trip over them when he tried to run.

Sebastian lived in a nice little house in the country with a little girl called "Skimpy" who was eight years old. Skimpy's mother and brother, Billy, also lived there. Skimpy didn't call her mother "mama" like most kids do. Instead she always called her mother "Mumpy".

Skimpy asked Mumpy if she could shave
Sebastian's whiskers so he could run without
tripping over them, but her mother said "no"
because she had never heard of anyone
shaving a cat's whiskers.

One day Skimpy got a great idea and decided to braid Sebastian's whiskers on each side of his face and then tie them together up on the back of his neck. She used a pretty little blue ribbon to tie them. Now, Skimpy thought, he can run and play without tripping over his whiskers.

It wasn't too long after Sebastian's whiskers were braided and tied together up on the back of his neck that Skimpy and Mumpy noticed that Sebastian seemed very tired during the day and wanted to sleep more than he usually did.

Well, there was something interesting going on at
night after the family had gone to bed. A little mouse
that lived in a little corner under the front porch had
gotten an idea when he saw Sebastian's braids.....
to the little mouse Sebastian kinda looked liked a
cowboy's horse when the cowboys put reins on them.
What if Mousie could ride Sebastian ... that would be
so much fun because he could sit on Sebastian's back
and hold onto the braids just like the cowboys held
onto the reins when they rode their horses.

One night Mousie tried to ride Sebastian
but he fell off. He decided if he had a saddle
he could stay on and not fall off, but where
could he get a saddle for a cat. Then he
remembered that Skimpy's brother, Billy, had
an old pair of tennis shoes and the tongue had
fallen off of one of the shoes. Why wouldn't
that work for a saddle?

So he found the tongue and a piece of
string and tied it on Sebastian's back. Wow! He
thought this looked great and it was just the
right size. So he jumped on Sebastian's back,
but after Sebastian ran just a little ways, Mousie
fell off again.

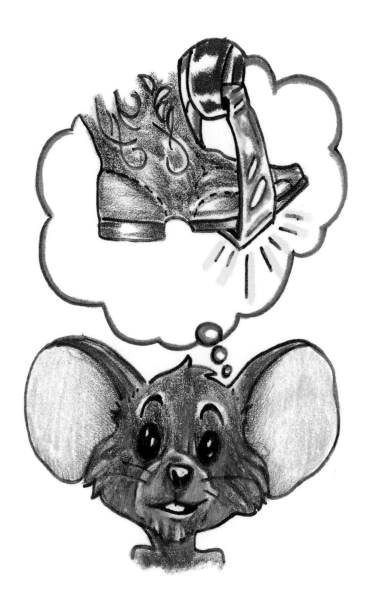

Now, Mousie realized that he needed some stirrups like the cowboys used so it would be easier for him to stay on Sebastian.

He thought about asking Billy if he knew where he could get some stirrups, but he remembered that Billy only liked toy cars and probably wouldn't know where to get them.

Mousie remembered that he saw Mumpy wearing some kind of loop earrings that might work as stirrups. Maybe if he knew where she kept her earrings, he could just borrow a pair. Sure enough that night when everyone was asleep he went into Mumpy's room and saw a box on her dresser and the lid was open.

Oh wow! When he looked inside there were lots of earrings. He saw a pair of silver loop earrings that were wider at the bottom which would be just right for his feet to fit into. So he borrowed the earrings and ran back down to his little corner under the front porch. He was so happy, because now he had everything he needed to try to be a real cowboy.

After he got the earrings hooked onto the
saddle, he remembered one more thing.

At Christmas-time someone had given Billy a
little cowboy doll with a cute cowboy hat. But
Billy never played with it because he only liked
playing with his toy cars.

So Mousie went back into the house and up
to Billy's room, and sure enough he found the
cowboy doll with the cowboy hat. He grabbed
the hat and rushed back down to his corner
under the front porch.

The rest of the night Mousie worked on hooking the stirrups on each side of the leather saddle which he had made from the tongue of Billy's tennis shoe. Then he tried on the little cowboy hat and it fit just right. Mousie was so excited. Maybe now he could be a real cowboy.

Now every night after Skimpy and Mumpy and Billy went upstairs to go to bed, Mousie would saddle up Sebastian and put on his cowboy hat and jump into the saddle so they could play cowboys and horses. They would run around on the front porch. Then they would ride through the little cat opening in the front door and ride all through the living room and dining room. They wouldn't go upstairs because they were afraid they would wake everyone up.

They had to keep their new adventures a secret.

Sebastian would run really fast and jump up
on the back of the couch. Then he would jump
up on the fireplace mantle. Mousie would hold
on tight to the whisker reins. He had to keep his
feet tight in the stirrups and also hold onto his
hat. He was so surprised that Sebastian could
run so fast and jump so high.

Just when Mousie would think that Sebastian was going to slow down, Sebastian would jump straight up onto a table or the back of a chair and then right back down.

Sometimes Mousie even felt a little scared, but he hung on as tight as he could so he wouldn't fall off.

Oh! This was so much fun and even Sebastian was surprised that Mousie could stay in the saddle without falling off. He really was a cowboy! And Sebastian was as good as any race horse. They had no idea that life could be so exciting. It was so fun!

Sebastian loved playing like a race horse. But the thing he liked the most was being able to run and jump without tripping over his whiskers. Now his whiskers really were like horse reins.

Every morning Mumpy's alarm went off at
6:00 o'clock and she would come downstairs to
make her coffee. Sebastian and Mousie knew
as soon as they heard the alarm go off they had
to stop playing cowboys and horses and
Mousie had to put the cowboy stuff away in his
little corner under the porch.

After Mumpy poured herself a cup of coffee she would then go out on the porch. She loved sitting in the swing on the front porch while she drank her coffee and listened to the birds sing.

Many times Sebastian who was very tired from
playing cowboys and horses all night would curl
up in Mumpy's lap and go to sleep.

And Mousie would go into his little corner under
the porch and snuggle up next to the saddle and
little cowboy hat and sleep while he dreamed of
playing more cowboy games.

So every night after everyone had gone upstairs to bed, Sebastian and Mousie knew they could start playing cowboys and horses again. It was their little secret.

It was so much fun!

It was wonderful!

* * * * *

So, Now You Know,
if a little mouse can become a cowboy,
you can be anything you want to be.

Made in the USA
Charleston, SC
16 December 2014